BUSY LIZZIE

by Holly Berry

North-South Books

NEW YORK / LONDON

Busy Lizzie
has two hands.

Clap your hands,
Busy Lizzie.

Busy Lizzie has two feet.

Kick your feet,
Busy Lizzie.

Busy Lizzie
has one nose.

Wiggle your nose, Busy Lizzie.

Busy Lizzie
has one belly.

Rub your belly,
Busy Lizzie.

Busy Lizzie
has two ears.

Tug your ears,
Busy Lizzie.

Busy Lizzie has one mouth.

Say good night,
Busy Lizzie.

Busy Lizzie has a warm bed.

Snuggle up...
sleep tight...Busy Lizzie.

Published in the United States by North-South Books Inc., New York.
Published simultaneously in Great Britain, Canada, Australia, and
New Zealand in 1994 by North-South Books, an imprint of
Nord-Süd Verlag AG, Gossau Zürich, Switzerland.
First paperback edition published in 1996.

Library of Congress Cataloging-in-Publication Data
Berry, Holly.
Busy Lizzie / by Holly Berry.
Summary: Busy Lizzie claps her hands, pulls her ears, and rubs her
belly in preparation for climbing into her warm bed and going to sleep.
[1. Bedtime—Fiction. 2. Play—Fiction.] I. Title.
PZ7.B46172BU 1994
[E]—DC20 94-5104

A CIP catalogue record for this book is available from The British Library.

*For more information about our books, and the authors and artists
who create them, visit our web site:* http://www.northsouth.com
The art for this book was prepared with colored pencils and watercolor.
Typography by Marc Cheshire. Calligraphy by Colleen
ISBN 1-55858-323-8 (TRADE BINDING)
1 3 5 7 9 TB 10 8 6 4 2
ISBN 1-55858-324-6 (LIBRARY BINDING)
1 3 5 7 9 LB 10 8 6 4 2
ISBN 1-55858-615-6 (PAPERBACK)
1 3 5 7 9 PB 10 8 6 4 2
Printed in Belgium